Dear Parents and Educators,

Welcome to Penguin Young Readers! As parents and educators, you know that each child develops at his or her own pace—in terms of speech, critical thinking, and, of course, reading. Penguin Young Readers recognizes this fact. As a result, each Penguin Young Readers book is assigned a traditional easy-to-read level (1–4) as well as a Guided Reading Level (A–P). Both of these systems will help you choose the right book for your child. Please refer to the back of each book for specific leveling information. Penguin Young Readers features esteemed authors and illustrators, stories about favorite characters, fascinating nonfiction, and more!

The Garden That We Grew

LEVEL 2

GUIDED READING LEVEL **H**

This book is perfect for a **Progressing Reader** who:
• can figure out unknown words by using picture and context clues;
• can recognize beginning, middle, and ending sounds;
• can make and confirm predictions about what will happen in the text; and
• can distinguish between fiction and nonfiction.

Here are some **activities** you can do during and after reading this book:
• Retelling: Have the child tell you what the story is about. When you're growing pumpkins, what happens at the beginning, middle, and end of the process?
• Rhyming Words: Have the child list all the rhyming words in the story. Write each word next to the word it rhymes with. Use the chart below as an example.

Word	Rhymes with
brown	down
grow	row
seeds	weeds

Remember, sharing the love of reading with a child is the best gift you can give!

—Bonnie Bader, EdM
  Penguin Young Readers program

*Penguin Young Readers are leveled by independent reviewers applying the standards developed by Irene Fountas and Gay Su Pinnell in *Matching Books to Readers: Using Leveled Books in Guided Reading*, Heinemann, 1999.

For Julie Hannah and her green thumb—JH

To my mother MN—HN

Penguin Young Readers
Published by the Penguin Group
Penguin Group (USA) Inc., 375 Hudson Street, New York, New York 10014, USA
Penguin Group (Canada), 90 Eglinton Avenue East, Suite 700, Toronto, Ontario M4P 2Y3, Canada
(a division of Pearson Penguin Canada Inc.)
Penguin Books Ltd., 80 Strand, London WC2R 0RL, England
Penguin Group Ireland, 25 St. Stephen's Green, Dublin 2, Ireland (a division of Penguin Books Ltd.)
Penguin Group (Australia), 250 Camberwell Road, Camberwell, Victoria 3124, Australia
(a division of Pearson Australia Group Pty. Ltd.)
Penguin Books India Pvt. Ltd., 11 Community Centre, Panchsheel Park, New Delhi—110 017, India
Penguin Group (NZ), 67 Apollo Drive, Rosedale, Auckland 0632, New Zealand
(a division of Pearson New Zealand Ltd.)
Penguin Books (South Africa) (Pty.) Ltd., 24 Sturdee Avenue,
Rosebank, Johannesburg 2196, South Africa

Penguin Books Ltd., Registered Offices: 80 Strand, London WC2R 0RL, England

Text copyright © 2001 by Joan Holub. Illustrations copyright © 2001 by Hiroe Nakata. All rights reserved.
First published in 2001 by Viking and Puffin Books, imprints of Penguin Group (USA) Inc. Published in
2012 by Penguin Young Readers, an imprint of Penguin Group (USA) Inc., 345 Hudson Street,
New York, New York 10014. Manufactured in China.

The Library of Congress has cataloged the Viking edition
under the following Control Number: 00010966

ISBN 978-0-14-131198-2   10 9 8 7 6 5 4 3 2 1

The Garden That We Grew

by Joan Holub
illustrations by Hiroe Nakata

Penguin Young Readers
An Imprint of Penguin Group (USA) Inc.

This is the garden
that we will grow.
This is the patch
we will plant row
by row.

This is the dirt,

all warm and brown.

These are the seeds
we push way down.

This is the water

we spray on the seeds.

These are our hands

that pull out the weeds.

These are the buds

that peek from their beds.

These are the flowers

that poke out their heads.

These are the pumpkins

that grow on the vine.

These are the summer days
filled with sunshine.

These are the worms

that go here and there.

These are the bees

that buzz in the air.

This is the day
we have all waited for.
We pick our pumpkins—
one, two, three, four!

Inside the pumpkins

is wet, orange goop.

This is the way

we scoop, scoop, scoop, scoop!

This is the pie

we make and we munch.

These are the cookies

we bake by the bunch.

These are the faces

that grin ear to ear.

Let's save the seeds . . .

to grow pumpkins next year!